THE

A NOVELLA

THE RECKONING

A NOVELLA

JAYDEN CARLISLE

to all of you that have supported me on my
writing journey,
Thank you for the support!

THE RECKONING

A NOVELLA

CHAPTER ONE
THE DAY BEFORE

On a scorching summer afternoon, with the mercury nearly hitting 80 degrees in the vibrant city of Miami, Florida, the calendar marked the 7th of June, 1997. Behind the wheel, Alex embarked on a journey to his best friend's lavish summer pool bash. As he navigated the streets, the sun blazed down upon the asphalt, painting the city in a golden hue. Despite the urgency to arrive at the festivity, Alex's heart skipped a beat as he realized he had left his inhaler behind. With a mere 30 minutes to reach the party and the closest pharmacy a ten-minute drive away, a sense of anxiety settled over him like a suffocating blanket. With determination etched in his features, Alex pushed his car forward, the minutes slipping away as he traversed the sun-drenched streets. However, his haste led him to disregard the speed limits, his speedometer climbing to sixty in a forty-five zone. It was then, just moments away from his destination, that the flashing lights of law enforcement danced in his rearview mirror.

"God dammit," Alex muttered under his breath, beads of sweat forming on his brow as he watched a figure clad in a khaki and dark brown uniform approach his window. Tinted aviators shielded the sheriff's eyes, adding an air of authority to his demeanor. With palpable tension in the air, Alex rolled down his window to face the sheriff's scrutiny.

"Son, did you realize you were going sixty in a forty-five?" the sheriff inquired, his tone firm yet measured. Feeling the weight of his urgency, Alex fabricated a story about his wife's supposed pregnancy, hoping to elicit some leniency from the law. However, the sheriff's skepticism lingered in his gaze as he probed further. Undeterred, Alex persisted with his ruse, the urgency of his fabricated situation palpable in his voice. After a brief exchange, the sheriff relented, granting Alex a reprieve with a warning to drive safely. As Alex hurriedly procured his inhaler from the pharmacy, time continued its relentless march forward, each passing second diminishing his window of punctuality. With a sense of urgency propelling him, he dashed back to his vehicle, determined to make up for lost time.

Finally arriving at the party, albeit a mere four minutes behind schedule, Alex was greeted by his best friend Logan with a warm smile. Amidst the jovial atmosphere, Alex settled in, exchanging pleasantries and catching up with old acquaintances. However, amidst the laughter and merriment, Alex's gaze was drawn to a familiar figure by the poolside – Vanessa, his high school crush, adorned the scene with her presence. Surprised by her attendance, Alex felt a rush of nerves coursing through him as he contemplated approaching her. Summoning his courage, Alex engaged Vanessa in conversation, his heart pounding with anticipation. Despite his initial apprehension, their interaction flowed effortlessly, punctuated by smiles and laughter.

As the evening wore on, Alex's anxiety gave way to a sense of ease in Vanessa's company. However, their tranquility was shattered by a sudden commotion emanating from Vanessa's tent. Rushing to her aid, Alex was met with a harrowing sight – an assailant attacking Vanessa with alarming ferocity.

Reacting swiftly, Alex intervened, confronting the assailant in a desperate bid to protect Vanessa. In the ensuing struggle, he found himself facing a foe unlike any other – a grotesque figure with pallid skin and haunting yellow eyes. With a mixture of horror and determination, Alex fought to defend Vanessa, his actions driven by instinct and adrenaline. It was only when he delivered a decisive blow to the head that the threat was neutralized, leaving the assailant lifeless at their feet.

In the aftermath of the harrowing encounter, Vanessa expressed her gratitude, her words echoing with sincerity. As they grappled with the aftermath of the ordeal, a newfound bond forged in the crucible of adversity, Alex and Vanessa found solace in each other's presence.

As the night became darker, that attack lingered in their minds, a somber reminder of the fragility of life. Yet, amidst the turmoil, a flicker of hope burned bright – a connection forged in the crucible of chaos, binding two souls together in a bond that transcended mere circumstance.

As the party continued in full swing. Laughter echoed around the pool, mingling with the faint sound of music playing in the background. Suddenly, amidst the festivities, a loud commotion erupted from the outskirts of the property.

"What's going on?" Alex muttered, his brows furrowing in concern. Logan, his eyes widening with alarm, pointed toward the edge of the woods surrounding the backyard.

"Look! Something's happening over there!"

A figure stumbled out of the darkness, its movements erratic and jerky. As it drew closer, the group's collective gasp filled the air. The person's skin was pallid, their eyes vacant and unfocused. A sickly, guttural moan emanated from their lips.

"Oh no," Vanessa whispered, her voice barely audible over the growing clamor.

Before they could react, more figures emerged from the shadows, each displaying the same disturbing symptoms. The realization dawned on them like a chilling wave—these were not ordinary party crashers; they were something else entirely.

"We need to get inside, now!" Alex exclaimed, his voice tinged with urgency. With adrenaline-fueled speed, the group rushed toward the house, their hearts pounding in their chests. They slammed the door shut behind them, barricading it with whatever makeshift barriers they could find.

"We're not safe here," Logan muttered, his eyes scanning the room for any signs of weakness in their defenses.

Outside, the sounds of shuffling footsteps grew louder, accompanied by the haunting moans of the infected. It was clear they were closing in, drawn by the scent of human flesh. Occasional thuds reverberated through the sturdy walls of the house, followed by sickening crunches and wet, tearing sounds that made their skin crawl. It was the sound of bodies being torn asunder, of bones snapping under the relentless onslaught of the infected horde. The air grew heavy with the acrid scent of blood and decay, seeping through the cracks and invading their senses with a nauseating intensity. Each anguished scream that pierced the night was a stark reminder of the grim reality unfolding just beyond their reach.

Frozen in fear, the group listened helplessly as the symphony of death played out in the darkness, their hearts heavy with the weight of the horrors they bore witness to. In that moment, they realized the true extent of the peril they faced, and the daunting challenge of surviving the night ahead.

"We need to find another way out," Alex said, his voice steady despite the rising panic within him. Frantically, they searched the house for an escape route, but their efforts proved futile. Trapped and surrounded, their only option was to fortify their position and wait for dawn to break.

As the night dragged on, the tension inside the house reached a fever pitch. Every creak of the floorboards, every distant moan sent shivers down their spines. They huddled together, their minds racing with fear and uncertainty. With the first light of dawn creeping through the windows, they knew they had survived the night. But outside, the infected still lurked, a grim reminder of the dangers that lay beyond their sanctuary. As they prepared to face whatever lay ahead, they knew one thing for certain—their fight for survival was far from over.

CHAPTER TWO
FORTIFY

As the group peered out the window, they saw a horde of infected slowly making their way towards the house. Panic began to set in as they realized the gravity of the situation.

"We need to fortify this place and make a plan," Alex said with a sense of urgency. Logan nodded in agreement. "We should gather whatever supplies we can and reinforce the doors and windows."

Vanessa chimed in, "We also need weapons. Something more than just a shotgun."

They quickly began searching the house for anything they could use as makeshift weapons and more barricades. Logan retrieved his father's gun while Alex and Vanessa gathered tools and furniture to reinforce the entrances. As they worked, the sound of banging on the front door grew louder. The infected were getting closer to the windows, and time was running out.

"We need to hurry!" Alex shouted over the noise. They worked frantically, adrenaline coursing through their veins as they fortified the house as best they could. Finally, they retreated to the second floor, hoping to find safety there. But their relief was short-lived. From the upstairs window, they could see the infected breaking through the barricades downstairs, pouring into the house like a flood.

"We need to go," Vanessa said, her voice trembling. Logan nodded, his expression grim.

"There's no other choice. We have to get out of here."

Alex scanned the room, his mind racing for a plan. Then, an idea struck him.

"The attic!" he exclaimed. "We can climb out the window onto the roof and make our way to the attic."

They wasted no time in executing the plan. With adrenaline-fueled speed, they climbed out the window and onto the roof, careful to avoid the grasping hands of the infected below. Once inside the attic, they huddled together, heartbeats thundering in their ears as they listened to the sounds of the infected below.

"We need to find a way out of here," Alex said, his voice low but determined. "But how?" Vanessa asked, her eyes wide with fear.

Logan's gaze flickered to a small window on the far side of the attic. "Through there," he said, pointing.

They nodded in silent agreement and made their way to the window. With trembling hands, they pushed it open and peered outside. Below them stretched the property, overrun with the infected.

"We'll have to jump," Alex said, his voice steady despite the fear coursing through him.

Without hesitation, they leaped from the window, landing hard on the ground below. Ignoring the pain, they scrambled to their feet and ran, the sounds of the infected echoing around them.

As they fled into the unknown, they knew one thing for certain: their fight for survival was far from over. The group ran through the desolate streets, their breaths ragged and their hearts pounding with adrenaline. They didn't stop until they reached the outskirts of the neighborhood, where they finally collapsed in exhaustion.

"We made it," Logan gasped, his chest heaving as he spoke.

"Yeah, but for how long?" Vanessa replied, her voice tinged with uncertainty. Alex glanced around at their surroundings, taking in the eerie silence that hung over the deserted streets. "We need to find somewhere safe to regroup and figure out our next move."

As they caught their breath, they scanned the area for any sign of shelter. Finally, they spotted an abandoned building nearby and made their way towards it. Inside, they found a relatively secure room and collapsed onto the floor, the weight of their ordeal finally catching up to them.

"We can't stay here forever," Logan said, breaking the silence that had settled over them.

"I know," Alex replied, his mind already turning to their next steps. "But for now, let's rest and gather our strength. Tomorrow, we'll figure out our next move."

With that, they settled in for the night, knowing that the road ahead would be fraught with danger and uncertainty. The group found a small truck with the keys still inside. It was also filled with gas. They got in and they traveled for hours until they stumbled upon a military base nestled in the outskirts of the city. As they approached the gates, armed guards greeted them cautiously.

"We come in peace," Alex announced, raising his hands in a sign of surrender. "We're just looking for a safe place to rest."

The guards eyed them suspiciously before one of them spoke into his radio, relaying their request. After a tense few moments, the gates slowly creaked open, allowing them entry.

Inside, they were met by Logan's father, a stern-looking man in military uniform who held a position of command at the base.

"Dad!" Logan exclaimed, rushing forward to embrace him. Logan's father returned the embrace briefly before pulling back to assess the group. "What brings you all here?" he asked, his tone serious.

"We're trying to find a safe place to stay," Alex replied. "We heard there might be safety here."

Logan's father nodded, understanding evident in his eyes. "You're welcome to stay," he said. "But you'll need to follow our rules and regulations."

"We understand," Vanessa replied, speaking for the group. "Thank you for letting us in."

With that, they were ushered inside the base, where they found temporary refuge among the military personnel. As they settled in, they couldn't help but feel a sense of relief knowing they were finally in a place where they could catch their breath and plan their next moves under the protection of Logan's father and his fellow soldiers.

Logan's father led the group to the sleeping quarters, a row of bunk beds neatly arranged in a large room. The scent of cleanliness and order greeted them as they entered.

"Make yourselves comfortable here," Logan's father instructed, gesturing to the beds. "Rest up. Tomorrow will be a busy day."

As they settled onto the soft mattresses, fatigue finally caught up with them. But before drifting off to sleep, they engaged in a conversation about the state of the world and the uncertainty of their future.

"Do you ever think, like... Is the world ever going to go back to normal?" Alex pondered aloud, breaking the silence that had settled over the group. Vanessa sighed, her expression reflective.

"I don't know," she admitted. "It's hard to imagine things ever being the same again after everything we've seen."

Logan's father, who had been quietly listening, spoke up.

"It's natural to wonder," he said. "But right now, our focus should be on surviving. We'll take it one day at a time and do whatever it takes to keep ourselves and others safe."

The group fell silent, each lost in their own thoughts as they contemplated the uncertain future that lay ahead. Eventually, exhaustion overtook them, and one by one, they succumbed to sleep, finding solace in the warmth of the beds and the temporary peace of the military base.

CHAPTER THREE
TOO SOON

The next morning, Alex woke up to the sound of birds chirping outside the quarters. He stretched his arms and looked around the room. The others were still asleep, so he decided to take a walk around the base to get a feel for their new surroundings. As he strolled through the compound, Alex noticed the organized chaos of military life. Soldiers were training, vehicles were being repaired, and supplies were being distributed. Despite the threat of the infected lurking outside, there was a sense of order and purpose within the base.

As Alex walked, he couldn't shake off the feeling of unease. The thought of the infection spreading closer to Phoenix weighed heavily on his mind. He knew they couldn't stay in the safety of the base forever. Eventually, they would have to venture out into the world again. Lost in his thoughts, Alex almost didn't notice the figure approaching him. It was Mandy, the general he had met the previous night.

"Good morning, Alex," Mandy greeted him with a nod.

"Morning, General," Alex replied, returning the nod. Mandy glanced around before speaking in a lowered voice.

"I need to talk to you about something important." Alex's curiosity piqued. "What is it?"

Mandy hesitated for a moment before continuing.

"I've received word from our scouts. The infected are closing in on Phoenix faster than we anticipated. It's only a matter of time before they breach our defenses."

Alex felt a knot form in his stomach.

"What do we do?"

Mandy looked at him gravely.

"We need to prepare for the worst. I've ordered a full evacuation of the base. We're relocating to a more secure location deeper inland."

Alex nodded, understanding the gravity of the situation. "When do we leave?"

"Soon. We're gathering supplies and organizing transport as we speak," Mandy replied. "I need you to rally your group and make sure they're ready to move at a moment's notice."

"I'll do it," Alex assured her.

"Good. We don't have much time," Mandy said, her expression serious. "Keep your eyes open and stay alert. The infected could strike at any moment."

With that, Mandy turned and walked away, leaving Alex deep in thought. He knew they were facing a dangerous journey ahead, but he was determined to lead his group to safety. Returning to the quarters, Alex woke up the others and relayed the news. They quickly packed their belongings and gathered in the courtyard, ready to depart.

As the chaos outside escalated, the group's sense of security dwindled with each passing moment. Despite their best efforts to fortify their defenses, the relentless onslaught of the infected threatened to breach their sanctuary.

Suddenly, with a deafening crash, the front gates gave way under the force of the infected horde. Panic erupted within the base as the group scrambled for safety, their hearts pounding with fear. In the midst of the chaos, Mandy, clutching a firearm in trembling hands, attempted to defend the group against the encroaching threat. But in the frenzy of the moment, a stray bullet ricocheted off the walls, striking Logan with a devastating blow.

Time seemed to stand still as Logan's father, horror etched upon his face, rushed to his son's side. With trembling hands, he cradled Logan's lifeless body, his heart breaking with each passing moment. Tears streamed down his cheeks as he whispered words of disbelief and anguish, mourning the loss of his beloved son. In that moment of profound grief, the weight of their shared loss hung heavy upon the group, their sorrow palpable in the air. In a blaze of fury and desperation, Logan's father rose to his feet, his eyes burning with righteous anger. With grim determination, he turned to face Mandy, the source of their unimaginable suffering. In a swift and decisive motion, he raised his weapon, the echoes of his son's final moments fueling his resolve. With a steady hand and unwavering determination, he took aim and delivered justice upon Mandy, the one responsible for tearing their world apart. As the echoes of the gunshot faded into the night, a solemn silence fell upon them, broken only by the sound of Logan's father's ragged breaths. In that moment, amidst the devastation and loss, a glimmer of vengeance was born—a testament to the unfathomable depths of human resilience in the face of unspeakable tragedy. As they boarded the transport vehicles, Alex looked around at his companions. With a sense of resolve, the group set off towards their next destination, leaving behind the overrun military base and venturing into the unknown once again. As they drove away, Alex couldn't help but wonder what lay ahead for them. But one thing was certain: they would face it together, as a team, come what may.

And so, their journey continued, with hope in their hearts and determination in their souls, as they forged ahead into the uncertain future that awaited them.

CHAPTER FOUR
THE PASSING

The night grew darker as the group broke off from the rest of the convoy and stopped for a late dinner, the weight of recent events heavy upon their hearts. Vanessa's inquiry pierced the silence, her concern palpable as she broached the topic that weighed heavily on Alex's mind. With each passing moment, the distant wail of sirens grew louder, a portent of impending chaos that loomed on the horizon. Alex's instincts propelled the group towards the source of the disturbance, their footsteps echoing the urgency that drove them forward.

Yet, their arrival at the scene of turmoil was met with chaos and confusion, their quest for answers thwarted by the cacophony of fear and panic that surrounded them. Logan's desperate search for his father ended in tragedy, his anguished cries were stuck replaying in Alex's head as Mandy's fatal mistake shattered his world.

In the aftermath of tragedy, grief enveloped the group, their mourning punctuated by the harsh reality of their grim existence.

As dawn broke, a sense of melancholy settled over the group, their journey marred by loss yet tempered by the flicker of hope that burned within their hearts. The unexpected transmission breathed new life into their weary souls, offering a glimmer of hope amidst the desolation that surrounded them. With their destination less than 6 hours away, the group set out once more, their resolve unbroken despite the trials that lay ahead. As they bid farewell to the old life that dragged behind, the promise of a new beginning beckoned on the horizon, a testament to the resilience of the human spirit amidst the darkness that threatened to engulf them.

CHAPTER FIVE

THE LONG DRIVE

The group's journey led them to a desolate gas station, a beacon of respite amidst the desolation that surrounded them.

"I have to pee," Said Vanessa.

"I'll accompany you, just to ensure everything's alright," Alex offered, his protective instincts guiding his actions.

As Vanessa attended to her needs, Alex ventured deeper into the almost untouched store, his senses alert to the possibility of sustenance amidst the remnants of civilization. To his astonishment, the store remained in pristine condition, its shelves brimming with provisions long forgotten by time. A sudden noise shattered the silence, prompting Alex to ready his defenses, his grip tightening around the handle of his knife as he slowly unsheathed it. A confrontation ensued as an old man, wielding a double barreled shotgun, emerged from the shadows, his gruff demeanor a testament to the hardships he endured. Alex's explanations faltered amidst the tension, his intentions questioned by the wary old man. Their exchange, fraught with uncertainty, culminated in a fragile alliance forg amidst the chaos that besieged them.

As Vanessa emerged from the bathroom, her warmth and kindness bridged the gap between strangers, offering solace amidst the uncertainty that shrouded their journey.

"Who are you?" Alex's voice echoed through the silence, his tone a mix of suspicion and curiosity. The old man, his eyes crinkling at the corners with a weary smile, regarded them with a mixture of amusement and wisdom.

"Names Otis," he replied in a gravelly voice that seemed to carry the weight of a lifetime's worth of stories.

Vanessa, her gaze softened by the warmth of the candlelight, took a step forward.

"What are you doing here, Otis?" she asked, her voice laced with genuine concern. Otis chuckled softly, the sound echoing through the dimly lit room like the comforting melody of a bygone era.

"This is my shop, missy," he replied, his words tinged with a hint of nostalgia. Otis nodded, his eyes twinkling with a hint of mischief.

"Lived here my whole life," he replied, his voice tinged with a sense of pride. "Seen more than my fair share of trials and tribulations."

Alex, his curiosity piqued by Otis's cryptic words, leaned in closer.

"What do you mean by that?" he asked, his voice barely above a whisper.

The old man's gaze grew distant, as if lost in the labyrinth of his own memories.

"Seen the world change, son," he replied, his voice tinged with a note of melancholy. "Seen the best of times and the worst of times."

As the group listened intently, Otis's words seemed to weave a tapestry of tales from a bygone era—a testament to the resilience of the human spirit in the face of adversity. And as they sat in the glow of the flickering candlelight, surrounded by the echoes of the past, they couldn't help but feel a sense of kinship with the old man named Otis—a reminder that, even in the darkest of times, there was still hope to be found in the unlikeliest of places. As the conversation with Otis unfolded, Alex and Vanessa exchanged a glance, silently communicating their shared sentiment. It was clear to them that Otis was more than just an old helpless man; he was a beacon of wisdom and experience in their time of need.

"Otis," Alex began tentatively, his voice filled with sincerity, "we're headed to a safer place, away from all this chaos. It's not far, and we could use someone like you with us."

Vanessa nodded in agreement, her eyes reflecting the genuine warmth in her heart. "You've seen so much, Otis," she added softly. "But there's safety in numbers, and we'd be honored to have you join us."

Otis regarded them both with a mixture of surprise and contemplation, his weathered features softened by their genuine offer of companionship. "I appreciate the offer, young'uns," he replied, his voice tinged with a hint of reluctance. "But I've owned this shop for nearly thirty years. It's been my home, my livelihood..."

Alex and Vanessa listened intently, understanding the weight of Otis's words. They knew that asking him to leave behind his life's work was no small request.

"But Otis," Vanessa interjected gently, her eyes alight with conviction, "there's safety in numbers. And besides, you've already done your fair share of surviving alone. Let us help you."

For a moment, a flicker of uncertainty crossed Otis's face, as if torn between the comfort of familiarity and the uncertainty of the unknown. But then, with a sigh that seemed to carry the weight of a lifetime of memories, he relented.

"Alright," he replied, his voice tinged with a mixture of resignation and gratitude. "I suppose a change of scenery couldn't hurt. Lead the way, young'uns. I'll follow."

And with that, as the group prepared to embark on their journey together, they couldn't help but feel a sense of hope stirring within them—a reminder that even in the darkest of times, the bonds of friendship and companionship could light the way forward. Their departure was hastened by distant gunfire, a grim reminder of the dangers that lurked beyond the safety of this old shop. With supplies in tow, they embarked once more upon their journey, their destination veiled in the promise of sanctuary amidst the chaos.

Nightfall descended, shrouding the landscape in an eerie cloak of darkness, punctuated by Alex's desperate encounter with an unknown assailant. Vanessa's swift intervention averted tragedy, her courage a beacon of hope amidst the encroaching darkness.

As dawn broke, they resumed their journey, their resolve unyielding in the face of adversity. A pit stop provided a brief respite, a chance to replenish their strength before pressing onward towards their destination. Yet, fate intervened once more as their vehicle faltered, its mechanical woes threatening to derail their journey.

The pungent stench of decay permeated the air, a grim reminder of the dangers that lurked in the shadows. Amidst the chaos, laughter echoed through the darkness, a fleeting moment of levity amidst the grim reality that surrounded them.

With each step, they drew closer to their destination, their spirits unbroken despite the trials that awaited them. Hand in hand, they marched forward, their bond forged in the crucible of adversity, a testament to the resilience of the human spirit.

CHAPTER SIX
SUPPLIES

As the group's journey to Morris Ranch in Texas neared its completion. They had traveled for miles on foot, navigating feet aching terrain and weathering the remnants of a world torn apart by chaos. But now, as they drew closer to their destination, a sense of anticipation filled the air.

Alex and Vanessa led the way, their eyes fixed on the horizon as they followed the guidance of the EVAC center run by Erick and his parents. Erick, a longtime family friend known for his resourcefulness and unwavering determination, served as their beacon of hope in these uncertain times.

The path stretched out before them, winding through the rugged landscape of the Texas countryside. As they walked, the conversation flowed freely between them, a mixture of laughter and camaraderie filling the air. They shared stories of their past adventures, reminiscing about the moments of triumph and hardship that had brought them to this point.

As the hours passed, the landscape gradually changed, giving way to the familiar sights of Morris Ranch. The air was filled with a sense of relief and anticipation as they neared their destination, their hearts buoyed by the promise of safety and sanctuary that awaited them at the EVAC center.

Finally, as the last rays of sunlight faded from the sky, they arrived at their destination, greeted by the warm embrace of Erick and his parents. With a sense of gratitude and relief, the group settled in, grateful for the journey that had brought them together and the hope that lay ahead. together, united in their quest for survival and the promise of a better tomorrow.

"That building resembles something out of a western movie," Vanessa remarked, her voice tinged with awe.

"It's a Rambler House," Otis interjected, his tone tinged with nostalgia. "I grew up in one of those."

"You a cowboy, then?" Vanessa's curiosity sparked an exchange of reminiscence.

"Once upon a time, I suppose. Now, just an old man," Otis chuckled, his laughter tinged with bittersweet reflection.

Erick's family, poised to depart in the morning aboard a waiting helicopter, became a beacon of reassurance amidst the chaos.

As dawn approached, the sky gradually lightened, painting the horizon with hues of pink and orange as the sun began to rise, casting its warm glow upon the group. The group deliberated their next course of action. They boarded the helicopter, settling upon a journey towards

Galveston, where rumors of survivor enclaves and military stockpiles beckoned.

Upon arrival, however, their optimism waned in the face of an overwhelming horde of infected, their collective resolve tested amidst the chaos.

As they prepared to depart, Alex's thoughts drifted towards the elusive promise of normalcy, his musings punctuated by Otis's mundane yet poignant declaration. As the helicopter soared through the sky, Otis shifted uncomfortably in his seat, his face contorted in discomfort.

"Hey, folks, hate to interrupt the ride, but nature's calling," Otis announced sheepishly, rubbing his hands together.

"No worries, Otis," Alex replied with a reassuring smile. "We'll land nearby to refuel anyway. Take your time."

As the helicopter descended to a clearing, Erick expertly guided the aircraft to a gentle landing, the whirling blades slowing to a halt. With a nod of gratitude, Otis unbuckled his seatbelt and made his way to the small bush around the back of an abandoned building.

"Alright, folks, we'll just be here for a few minutes," Erick announced over the intercom. "Time for a quick refuel." While the others prepared to refuel the helicopter, Otis emerged from the bathroom compartment with a sigh of relief, a sheepish grin on his face.

Suddenly, a guttural scream pierced the air, sending a chill down Alex's spine. He turned to see Otis, his face contorted in terror, as he stumbled backward, surrounded by a horde of infected.

"Otis!" Alex shouted, his heart pounding in his chest.

Without hesitation, Alex unbuckled his seatbelt and rushed to Otis's side, but it was too late. The infected descended upon him like a swarm of locusts, tearing into his flesh with savage ferocity.

"Get off of him!" Alex yelled, his fists swinging wildly as he fought to push back the encroaching horde. But the infected were relentless, their hunger insatiable as they ripped and tore at Otis's body, their bloodlust driving them into a frenzy.

"Alex, we have to go!" Vanessa cried, her voice filled with urgency as she grabbed his arm and pulled him back toward the helicopter.

Reluctantly, Alex tore his gaze away from the grisly scene unfolding before him, his heart heavy with grief and rage.

As the helicopter lifted off into the sky, leaving behind the nightmare below, Alex couldn't shake the image of Otis's final moments from his mind. It was a harsh reminder of the brutal reality they faced, and the fragility of life in a world consumed by darkness.

"If only I hadn't insisted that Otis come with us," Alex thought bitterly, his heart heavy with the weight of remorse. "Maybe he would still be alive and safe at his shop."

He couldn't shake the feeling that he had failed Otis, that his decision to bring him along had ultimately led to his demise. The thought gnawed at him, filling him with a sense of overwhelming guilt.

"I should have known better," Alex muttered to himself, his words lost amidst the roar of the helicopter's engine. "I should have protected him."

But deep down, Alex knew that hindsight offered little solace in the face of tragedy. Otis was gone, and no amount of regret could change that.

As the helicopter continued its journey toward safety, Alex vowed to honor Otis's memory by staying vigilant and protecting those he cared about. It was the least he could do to make amends for the mistake that had cost Otis his life. Alex snapped back out of his thoughts, only to see Vanessa sobbing over the loss of their new friend Otis.

"We must press on," Alex's voice, a whispered vow amidst the sadness, in which filled the confines of the helicopter. "There is no time for mourning. Our survival depends on it."

As they soared into the uncertain abyss of the unknown, Alex's resolve hardened, his determination a beacon of hope amidst the encroaching darkness.

CHAPTER SEVEN
BEFORE

Home. The word echoed in Alex's mind, a poignant reminder of what once was. Before the chaos descended, he resided with his uncle Marty in a quaint cottage nestled just beyond the outskirts of Miami. Yet, home was an illusory sanctuary, tainted by the specter of alcoholism that plagued Marty. His uncle's absence, a consequence of perpetual inebriation, left Alex to navigate the tumult of solitude. Days bled into nights, each moment fraught with the weight of unspoken despair. Marty's descent into alcohol-fueled oblivion culminated in a tragic episode, a drunken outburst mistaken for aggression towards Alex. The wounds inflicted were not merely physical; they seared deeper, etching scars upon Alex's soul. Yet, he remained tethered to the hope of redemption, an unspoken vow to mend what was fractured. The shadow of Alex's father loomed large, casting a pall over their fractured familial dynamic. Incarcerated for a heinous crime, his absence reverberated through the halls of their shared memory, a reminder of the tenuous thread that bound them together.

Moments of solace were fleeting, punctuated by Marty's erratic behavior. Even in the company of friends like Logan, their sanctuary was transient, shattered by Marty's unpredictable temper. Still, Alex clung to the shards of familial love, his devotion unwavering in the face of adversity.

News of Marty's demise arrived as a devastating blow, shattering the fragile semblance of stability that remained. In death, Marty transcended the confines of his affliction, leaving Alex adrift in a sea of unresolved grief. He was a beacon of solace in a world rife with uncertainty, a surrogate father figure whose absence left a profound void.

Amidst the chaos that engulfed their world, Alex harbored a flicker of hope - a hope that transcended the boundaries of reality. Thoughts of his father, shrouded in the enigma of his fate, haunted his restless nights. Yet, amidst the cacophony of despair, a beacon of optimism illuminated his path, guiding him towards the elusive promise of reunion.

The deafening roar of the helicopter drowned out Alex's inquiries, rendering his voice a mere whisper amidst the tumultuous thrum of the rotors.

"Where are we headed?" Alex's voice reverberated, strained against the cacophony of the aircraft's engines.

"What?" Erick's response, barely audible above the din, elicited a frustrated outburst from Alex.

"Where are we going?" His query, amplified by urgency, punctuated the oppressive silence.

"We're scouting for a suitable location to establish camp before nightfall," Erick's response, tinged with urgency, conveyed the gravity of their mission. With fuel reserves dwindling, Erick skillfully navigated the helicopter towards a makeshift landing site near the border of Virginia and North Carolina. The open expanse of the field beckoned, offering a temporary respite from the relentless onslaught of their journey.

Surveying their surroundings, the group alighted upon an abandoned edifice, its weathered facade a testament to the passage of time. Within its dilapidated confines, they glimpsed the potential for renewal - a canvas upon which they could weave the threads of resilience and fortitude.

"We can make this place our home," Alex proclaimed, his voice infused with determination. With purposeful resolve, they set about fortifying their newfound sanctuary, laboring tirelessly to fortify its defenses against the encroaching darkness.

"By the way, I'm Christa, and this is Jack," Erick's mother's introduction, a gesture of camaraderie amidst adversity, offered a glimmer of solace amidst the chaos.

CHAPTER EIGHT

SAFE

Three months had elapsed since the intrepid group had settled into their newfound sanctuary. Their stronghold, fortified with a collection of armaments, now stood as an impregnable bastion. Amidst the security measures, they had cultivated verdant fields and unearthed an old generator, a relic now harnessed to provide essential power. The plumbing system flowed seamlessly, a testament to their collective ingenuity.

While the morning sun bathed the enclave in a golden hue, Alex and Vanessa sat alongside Erick's parents, indulging in a modest breakfast. Erick, their valiant scout, ventured beyond the perimeters on a mission to secure provisions - weapons, garments, and sustenance alike.

"Erick's been absent for an extended stretch. Do you reckon all's well?" Vanessa's concern echoed through the room.

"I have faith in his resilience. He's proven himself time and time again," Christa reassured, her voice imbued with maternal confidence.

"That's my boy. He'll return unscathed, mark my words," Jack affirmed, his paternal pride evident.

"Excuse me, I must attend to the farms," Alex interjected, rising from the table.

"Vanessa, care to lend a hand?" he invited, extending an offer for camaraderie.

Venturing to tend the agricultural plots, Alex's discerning eye discerned a troubling anomaly - the tomatoes bore unmistakable signs of intrusion, human teeth marks marred their once pristine surfaces. Urgency spurred action as Alex swiftly armed himself with a .45 ACP Colt 1911 handgun procured during a previous foray with Erick.

"Vanessa, hasten back inside and summon the others. We have an unwelcome visitor in our midst," Alex instructed, his tone resolute. Emboldened by resolve, he traversed the premises, issuing a stern challenge to the unseen intruder.

"Reveal yourself, coward! I am aware of your presence!" Alex's voice reverberated with authority.

His senses attuned, Alex detected faint footfalls emanating from the depths of the basement. Illuminating the cavernous space, he confronted the source of the disturbance - a waiflike figure, scarcely a child, cowered behind a weathered shelf. The boy, emaciated and unkempt, bore the unmistakable signs of neglect.

Approaching with cautious tenderness, Alex extended solace to the trembling child, his heart heavy with empathy.

The boy, bereft of trust, regarded him with wary curiosity, his haunting gaze betraying a harrowing past.

"Are you hungry, little one?" Alex's voice, laced with compassion, sought to assuage the boy's apprehension. Vanessa, accompanied by Erick's parents, descended into the basement, their expressions a tableau of disbelief at the sight before them.

"Poor soul," Christa murmured, her maternal instincts stirring her to action. Scooping the child into her arms, she ushered him indoors, her resolve unwavering in the face of adversity.

"I'll tend to this young soul's needs. Meanwhile, ensure those tomatoes are tended to, and mind you, wipe your feet before entering the house," she directed, her tone firm yet nurturing.

Exchanging a knowing glance, Alex and Vanessa stifled laughter, their bond fortified amidst the chaos.

"Very well, mother," Alex jestingly acquiesced, his playful banter a testament to their enduring camaraderie.

As dusk descended, heralding the end of another day, Erick returned bearing not only provisions but an unexpected addition to their ranks - a golden-coated Labrador pup, its endearing innocence a balm to their weary souls.

"A puppy!" Vanessa exclaimed, her delight palpable as she cradled the newfound companion. In the ensuing exchange, Alex seized the opportunity to confide in Erick, recounting the encounter with the enigmatic child discovered within the confines of their sanctuary. Erick's response, steeped in apprehension, bore witness to the grim reality of their predicament.

"So, you brought a potential threat into our midst, oblivious to the risks?" Erick's tone, laced with righteous indignation, betrayed his simmering discontent.

"Erick, he's but a child in need of our aid. To abandon him would be an affront to our humanity," Alex countered, his conviction unwavering in the face of opposition. Their discord, a testament to the moral quandaries that beset them, underscored the precarious balance between survival and compassion. Tempers flared as Erick, grappling with inner turmoil, retreated in silence, seeking solace in the familiarity of familial bonds.

As evening descended, casting an ethereal glow upon the landscape, Alex and Vanessa found solace in each other's embrace, their shared resolve a beacon of hope amidst uncertainty.

"Hey, Alex?" Vanessa's voice, soft yet resolute, broke the tranquility of the night.

"Yes, Nessa?" Alex's reply, infused with tenderness, mirrored the depths of his affection.

"What shall we name our newfound friend?" Vanessa inquired, her gaze alight with anticipation.

A moment of contemplation ensued before Alex, with a tender smile, offered a suggestion, his heart brimming with newfound warmth.

"Let's call him, Prudence." Alex suggested with a bright smile

She leaned in, her touch a testament to their unspoken bond, sealing their shared decision with a gentle kiss.

"Sounds perfect," she whispered, her voice a melody of contentment.

As the night unfolded, enveloping them in its embrace, Alex and Vanessa surrendered to the embrace of slumber, their hearts entwined in a tapestry of hope and resilience.

CHAPTER NINE
STRANGERS

The following morning dawned with a soft, golden light filtering through the dense canopy of trees that surrounded Alex and Vanessa's secluded refuge. As they finished their breakfast, the air was alive with the gentle hum of insects and the distant chirping of birds.

Taking advantage of the tranquil morning, Alex and Vanessa embarked on a leisurely stroll around the perimeter of their home, meticulously inspecting the sturdy fences that encircled their sanctuary. With every step, they scanned the horizon for any signs of intrusion, yet the tranquil landscape remained undisturbed.

"It's been three months now, and still not a soul in sight. Not even a whisper of movement," Vanessa remarked, her voice carrying a hint of disbelief.

"Let's not tempt fate, Nessa. We know they'll come eventually. It's just a matter of time," Alex replied, his tone tinged with a sense of urgency. "That's why we must remain vigilant and prepare ourselves for whatever may come."

Drawing closer to the heart of their homestead, Alex settled beside Erick, a lingering question weighing heavily on his mind.

"I've been meaning to ask you something," Alex began, his voice betraying a hint of curiosity. "Back at the EVAC center, why were we the only ones there?"

Erick's gaze shifted momentarily, his features clouded with a mix of memories and emotions. "The others? They evacuated the day before your arrival. Headed off to Vegas, they did. Another military outpost, they said," he explained, his voice trailing off.

"But why wait for us? Why risk your own safety?" Alex pressed, his curiosity unabated.

Erick's response was curt, his irritation palpable. Rising to his feet, he retreated to tend to the crops, leaving Alex to ponder his unanswered questions.

As the sun climbed higher in the sky, a distant rumble of thunder echoed across the landscape, heralding the approach of an ominous storm. Hastening indoors, Alex peered through the window, his gaze drawn to the gathering clouds rolling on the horizon.

"It's coming," he warned, his voice laced with urgency as he relayed the impending danger to his companions.

Moments later, a frantic pounding reverberated through the sturdy wooden door, the sound echoing eerily in the silence of the storm.

"Someone's at the door," Vanessa observed, her voice trembling with apprehension.

"Or something," Alex added grimly, his hand instinctively reaching for the reassuring weight of Otis's shotgun.

With each cautious step, Alex's heart thudded in his chest, his senses tuned to every creak of the floorboards beneath his feet. As he reached the door, he paused, his hand hovering over the doorknob, hesitating before he dared to peer through the peephole. What he saw sent a jolt of apprehension through him - three figures stood on the other side: a man, a woman, and a small child, their silhouettes illuminated by the dim light from the porch.

"It's a family," he murmured to himself, his grip tightening on the shotgun he held at his side. His mind raced with questions, suspicions bubbling to the surface as he braced himself to confront the unexpected visitors.

Summoning his resolve, Alex swung the door open, the metallic click of the shotgun echoing in the tense silence of the night. His eyes narrowed as he trained the weapon on the strangers before him, his voice firm as he demanded answers to the questions burning in his mind.

Their pleas for sanctuary washed over him, mingling with the howling wind outside. Despite the urgency in their voices, Alex's mistrust held firm, skepticism etched into the lines of his face. But as the storm raged on, pounding against the windows with relentless fury, a flicker of doubt crept into his thoughts. With a sigh, Alex relented, stepping aside to allow them temporary refuge within the shelter of his home. Yet, even as he did so, a sense of unease lingered in the air, thickening with each passing moment.

As the hours wore on, tensions simmered beneath the surface, a palpable tension hanging heavy in the air. The fragile peace they had managed to cling to shattered with a single, violent act. In a moment of shocking brutality, the strangers turned on Erick's father, their betrayal staining the floorboards with crimson.

"No... Dad!" Erick's cry pierced the air, his voice trembling with a mixture of fear and anguish. Alex's heart pounded in his chest as he watched in horror. Without hesitation, he lunged forward, his fingers tightening around the shotgun. Adrenaline surged through his veins as he raised the weapon, aiming it at the assailants with steely determination.

But before he could act, the father's voice cut through the chaos, a desperate plea for mercy.

"Please... don't..."

The plea fell on deaf ears as the strangers moved with ruthless efficiency. With a swift motion, the man raised a gleaming blade, the metallic glint of it catching the dim light as he plunged it into the father's chest. The sickening sound of flesh meeting steel echoed through the room, mingling with Erick's anguished cries. Time seemed to slow as Alex watched helplessly, his muscles tensing with the urge to intervene. But as Jack fell to the ground, life draining from his eyes, something inside Alex snapped. With a primal roar, he surged forward, the shotgun becoming an extension of his fury. He fired round after round, each shot a thunderous roar that reverberated through the room.

The attackers staggered back, caught off guard by the ferocity of Alex's onslaught. In the chaos that ensued, Erick joined the fray, his fists flying as he unleashed his pent-up rage upon the assailants.

Blood sprayed across the room as the battle raged on, a symphony of violence and desperation. And amidst the chaos, Alex and Erick fought with a single-minded purpose - to avenge the father they had lost, to reclaim the shattered remnants of their shattered lives.

When the dust finally settled, silence descended upon the room, broken only by the ragged gasps of the wounded and the steady drumming of rain against the windows. And as Alex and Erick stood amidst the carnage, their chests heaving with exertion, they knew that the battle was far from over. But for now, they had emerged victorious, their bond forged in blood and fire, stronger than ever before.

In the aftermath of the chaos, as the night stretched on in a haunting symphony of silence, each member of their makeshift family grappled with the weight of their actions. They were left to confront the harsh realities of a world consumed by darkness and despair.

As the moon cast its pale glow over the sleeping landscape, enveloping the world in a shroud of silence, Erick stirred from his slumber, his senses sharpened by a primal instinct that something was amiss.

With a heavy heart, he noticed the absence of his mother's comforting presence beside him. Yet, it was the peculiar absence of his father's lifeless form that sent a chill coursing down his spine. Suppressing the rising tide of unease, he reasoned that his mother must have ventured out to give his father a proper burial in the stillness of the night.

But as he ventured through the dimly lit corridors of their home, a nagging thought clawed at the edges of his consciousness.

"We didn't get the head," he muttered to himself in a sudden realization, the weight of his omission bearing down upon him like a leaden weight.

Rushing to the security of the gun cabinet, Erick's fingers closed around the cold steel of his father's revolver, his heart pounding in his chest as he braced himself for what lay ahead. With wary steps, he embarked on a desperate search for his mother, the eerie silence of the night punctuated only by the soft shuffle of his footsteps.

Yet, as he combed every inch of their refuge, a growing sense of dread settled over him like a suffocating blanket. The only remnant of violence remained in the lifeless form of the woman, man and daughter they had killed, her vacant gaze a chilling testament to the horrors that had unfolded. Fearing the worst, Erick's frantic search led him to the basement, where the darkness seemed to swallow him whole as he descended into its depths. With each step, his pulse quickened, his breaths coming in ragged gasps as he struggled to maintain his composure.

Then, cutting through the oppressive stillness like a knife, he heard it—a blood-curdling scream that tore through the silence, reverberating off the walls of the basement with a haunting intensity.

"Ma!" Erick's voice echoed in the darkness, laden with desperation and fear. "Where are you, Ma?" he cried out into the void, his words swallowed by the oppressive silence that surrounded him.

Yet, as he strained against the darkness, a flicker of movement caught his eye—a glimmer of light dancing on the edge of his vision. With newfound resolve, he sprinted toward the source of the sound, his footsteps echoing in the cavernous space as he chased after the elusive specter of his mother's voice. As Erick stood in the dimly lit basement, his heart hammered against his chest like a prisoner desperate to escape. The stench of decay hung heavy in the air, mingling with the metallic tang of blood. His father, Jack, once a pillar of strength and warmth, now stood before him, transformed into a grotesque caricature of his former self. Sunken eyes gleamed with hunger, his skin a sickly shade of gray, and tattered clothes hanging loosely from his emaciated frame.

"Erick, son, please," Jack's voice rasped, barely recognizable through the gurgles and growls that punctuated his words. "You know what you have to do."

Erick's hands trembled at his sides, his fingers wrapped tightly around the cold steel of the revolver. He couldn't bring himself to look directly at the creature that had once been his father. Memories flooded his mind: fishing trips, bedtime stories, laughter around the dinner table. But now, all that remained was a shell, a vessel overrun by the virus that had consumed so many.

"I can't," Erick whispered, his voice barely audible above the sound of his own heartbeat. "I can't do it, Dad. I can't..."

Tears welled in Erick's eyes, blurring his vision as he struggled to maintain his composure. Faced with the reality of the situation, he found himself paralyzed by grief and fear.

Jack lurched forward, his outstretched arms clawing at the air as he advanced towards his son.

"Erick, listen to me," he pleaded, his voice tinged with desperation. "You have to be strong. You have to do what needs to be done. I love you, son. But I'm not your father anymore. I'm just... a monster."

Erick's resolve hardened as he heard those words, his grip on the revolver tightening. He knew what he had to do, even if every fiber of his being rebelled against it. With a shaky breath, he raised the gun, his hands steady despite the turmoil raging within him.

"I love you too, Dad," Erick whispered, his voice cracking with emotion. "I'm sorry."

Time seemed to stand still as Erick squeezed the trigger, the deafening roar of the gunshot echoing through the basement. The bullet tore through the air, finding its mark with chilling accuracy. Jack's body jerked violently as the force of the impact sent him sprawling to the ground, lifeless eyes staring blankly at the ceiling.

Erick sank to his knees, the weight of his actions crushing him like a ton of bricks. Tears streamed down his cheeks as he cradled the revolver in his trembling hands, the echoes of his father's final words ringing in his ears. In that moment, he knew that he had lost more than just a parent. He had lost a piece of himself, forever tainted by the horrors of the world they now inhabited.

The next morning dawned with a somber stillness that hung heavy in the air, the aftermath of the previous night's violence lingering like a specter in the dim light filtering through the windows. Erick emerged from his fitful sleep with a heavy heart, the memory of his father's final moments haunting his dreams. With weary steps, he made his way downstairs, where his mother and the rest of the group had already gathered, their faces drawn with grief.

As they stood together in the cold light of morning, a sense of solemn purpose settled over them. In the center of the room lay the lifeless form of Erick's father, draped in a simple shroud of cloth. Around him, makeshift candles flickered, casting long shadows that danced across the walls.

Erick's mother stood beside the makeshift altar, her eyes red-rimmed with tears as she clutched a small bundle of wildflowers to her chest. Beside her, Alex stood tall and resolute, his expression a mask of grim determination as he surveyed the gathered group.

With a heavy sigh, Erick's mother began to speak, her voice thick with emotion as she shared memories of her beloved husband. She spoke of his kindness, his strength, and the love he had always shown for his family. As she spoke, tears streamed down her cheeks, mingling with the rain that pattered against the windows.

One by one, the others joined in, sharing their own stories and anecdotes about their time spent with Erick's father, over the last few months. They spoke of his bravery in the face of danger, his unwavering loyalty to those he loved, and the countless lives he had touched with his generosity and compassion.

As the tales flowed freely, grief gave way to a bittersweet sense of solace, a reminder of the profound impact Erick's father had made on those around him. And as the final words were spoken, the group gathered around the makeshift altar, their heads bowed in a silent prayer for the soul of the departed.

With trembling hands, Erick's mother placed the bundle of wildflowers atop the shroud, a final tribute to the man they had lost. And as the first rays of sunlight broke through the clouds, illuminating the room with a soft golden glow, they knew that though he may be gone, Erick's father would live on in their memories, a beacon of hope and inspiration in the darkness that lay ahead.

CHAPTER TEN
GONE

The morning sun filtered weakly through the heavy clouds, casting a pallid light over the somber scene that unfolded in the aftermath of the burial. With heavy hearts, Erick, his mother, and the rest of the group gathered in the dimly lit living room, their eyes still rimmed with traces of tears from the emotional farewell they had just bid to Erick's father.

Despite the weight of grief that hung in the air, a quiet determination settled over the group as they sought to find solace in each other's company. Alex, his usual stoicism softened by the events of the previous night, moved among them with quiet reassurance, his presence a source of strength amidst the uncertainty that loomed over their small sanctuary.

As they settled into a tentative rhythm, the remnants of the storm that had battered their home throughout the night began to recede, leaving behind a sense of eerie calm. Outside, the world seemed to hold its breath, as if waiting with bated anticipation for what would come next. For Erick and his companions, the road ahead remained uncertain, fraught with dangers both seen and unseen.

As the days passed and life settled into a new rhythm, Erick found himself drawn to the routine of hunting with Alex. It was a way to escape the suffocating weight of grief that still lingered in the air, if only for a few fleeting hours. And so, on a crisp morning several days after the burial, Erick and Alex set out into the wilderness surrounding their makeshift sanctuary, their footsteps muffled by the soft earth beneath their boots. The forest stretched out before them, a tapestry of greens and browns that seemed to breathe with life. The air was cool and fresh, tinged with the scent of damp earth and pine, as they ventured deeper into the heart of the wilderness. With practiced ease, Alex led the way, his movements fluid and sure as he navigated the winding paths that crisscrossed the forest floor. Erick followed close behind, his senses alive to the myriad sights and sounds that surrounded them.

As they walked, the conversation flowed easily between them, a welcome distraction from the weight of their shared grief. They spoke of their families, of the lives they had led before the world had been torn asunder by chaos and violence. They shared stories and anecdotes, laughter mingling with the rustle of leaves overhead. But beneath the surface, there lingered a sense of unease, a silent acknowledgment of the dangers that lurked beyond the safety of their sanctuary. They spoke in hushed tones of the rumors that had reached their ears - of marauders and bandits who roamed the wilderness, preying on the vulnerable and the unsuspecting.

As they walked, their senses remained on high alert, scanning the dense undergrowth for any sign of movement. The forest seemed to close in around them, the shadows growing deeper with each passing moment. But still, they pressed on, their determination unwavering in the face of adversity.

And so, as the day wore on and the sun began its slow descent towards the horizon, Erick and Alex continued their hunt, their footsteps echoing through the silent forest. Together, they forged ahead into the unknown, bound by a shared purpose and a steadfast resolve to survive in a world that had become all too unforgiving.

The gentle rustle of leaves, the distant call of birds, every nuance of the wilderness whispered secrets to them as they traversed the wooded terrain.

Suddenly, a flicker of movement caught Alex's eye. He raised a hand, motioning for Erick to halt, his gaze fixed intently on a clearing ahead. There, bathed in dappled sunlight, stood a majestic buck, its antlers reaching towards the sky in silent defiance.

Erick's breath caught in his throat as he followed Alex's line of sight, his heart pounding with anticipation. The deer stood perfectly still, its chestnut coat shimmering in the golden light, unaware of the danger that lurked nearby.

With a silent exchange of understanding, Alex nodded to Erick, his eyes alight with determination. Slowly, he raised his rifle, finger poised on the trigger as he took aim at the quarry.

The anticipation thickened the air, the forest around them hushing to witness the moment. Alex steadied his breath, the weight of the rifle familiar in his hands. With a surge of resolve, he pressed his finger against the trigger.

A sharp crack split the silence, echoing through the trees. The shot rang out, cutting through the stillness as the bullet found its mark. It was Alex who had fired, his aim true as the deer fell, a testament to his skill amidst the quiet expanse of the woods. The deer stumbled, a pained cry escaping its lips as it collapsed to the ground, the life draining from its eyes. Erick and Alex approached cautiously, their hearts heavy with the weight of what they had done. But they knew that this was the way of the world now, survival demanded sacrifice, and they were no strangers to its harsh realities. Together, they hoisted the deer onto their shoulders, its weight a solemn reminder of the delicate balance between life and death. With steady determination, they made their way back to their sanctuary, the fading light of day guiding their path through the forest.

When they returned home, Erick's mother greeted them with a mixture of relief and sadness, her eyes lingering on the deer slung between them. With a heavy heart, she set to work, her hands deftly skinning and gutting the animal with practiced precision.

Beside her, Vanessa lent a hand, her expression solemn as she assisted with the grim task at hand. Together, they worked in silence, the only sound the soft scrape of knives against flesh and bone.

As the evening wore on, the aroma of roasting meat filled the air, mingling with the scent of herbs and spices. Erick's mother worked tirelessly over the fire, her movements fluid and sure as she prepared a meal fit for a king.

And when the feast was finally ready, they gathered together around the rough-hewn table, their faces illuminated by the warm glow of the fire. With bowed heads and grateful hearts, they gave thanks for the bounty that had been provided, a testament to the resilience of the human spirit in the face of adversity.

Erick's mother presided over the meal, her expression a mixture of weariness and determination as she served each plate with loving care. Beside her, Vanessa moved with graceful efficiency, her hands deftly passing bowls of steaming vegetables and crusty bread.

As they ate, their laughter mingled with the crackle of flames, a fleeting moment of joy amidst the chaos that surrounded them. And as they raised their glasses in a silent toast to their fallen comrades and the uncertain future that lay ahead, they knew that as long as they had each other, they would find a way to weather whatever storms may come.

But amidst the laughter and camaraderie, there lingered an undercurrent of tension, a silent acknowledgment of the dangers that lurked beyond the safety of their sanctuary.

Erick's mother watched her son with a mixture of pride and concern, her eyes lingering on the weary lines etched into his face.

"You've been through so much, my dear," she said softly, reaching out to brush a stray lock of hair from his forehead. "But you mustn't lose hope. We'll get through this together, I promise."

Erick nodded, a small smile tugging at the corners of his lips as he met his mother's gaze. "I know, Mom," he replied, his voice thick with emotion. "We'll get through this, no matter what."

As the meal drew to a close, Alex rose from the table, a mischievous glint in his eye as he reached out to take Vanessa's hand. "Shall we retire for the evening, my dear?" he asked, his voice low and husky with desire.

Vanessa's cheeks flushed pink as she nodded, her hand tightening around Alex's as they made their way towards the stairs. Erick watched them go with a pang of envy, his heart heavy with longing for the kind of love and companionship they shared.

But as he turned back to his mother, he found solace in the warmth of her embrace, the love shining in her eyes a beacon of hope in the darkness that surrounded them. And as they settled in for the night, their hearts filled with gratitude for the blessings they had been given, they knew that no matter what trials may come, they would face them together, a family united in love and determination.

The following morning broke with a gentle light filtering through the windows, casting a soft glow over the small sanctuary that Erick and his companions called home. As the first rays of dawn painted the sky in hues of pink and gold, the household stirred to life, the sounds of morning filling the air with a sense of renewed energy.

Erick awoke to the comforting warmth of the blankets wrapped around him, the events of the previous night still fresh in his mind. Stretching languidly, he sat up in bed, rubbing the sleep from his eyes as he took in the familiar surroundings of his room.

Downstairs, the smell of breakfast filled the air, mingling with the sound of laughter and conversation as his companions gathered around the table. With a smile, Erick rose from his bed, eager to join them in the simple pleasures of a shared meal.

As he descended the stairs, he found his mother and Vanessa already deep in conversation, their voices rising and falling in animated discussion. They spoke of the future of their home, of plans for expansion and fortification to better withstand the dangers that lurked beyond their doorstep.

Erick listened with keen interest, his heart swelling with pride at the strength and determination of the women who had become his family.

But as the conversation turned to more personal matters, Erick sensed a shift in the air, a tension that lingered beneath the surface. With a discreet glance, he caught sight of Alex and Vanessa exchanging furtive glances, their expressions guarded as they spoke in hushed tones.

Curiosity piqued, Erick leaned in closer, straining to catch snippets of their conversation. But their words were lost to him, drowned out by the noise of the bustling household around them. As breakfast drew to a close, Alex and Vanessa rose from the table, their eyes meeting in a silent exchange of understanding. With a nod, they slipped away from the group, disappearing into the privacy of their shared room.

Alone at last, they spoke in hushed tones, their voices low and intimate as they broached the subject that had been weighing heavily on their minds. They spoke of their love for one another, of their hopes and dreams for the future.

And then, in a moment of quiet revelation, they spoke of the possibility of starting a family of their own, of bringing new life into a world that had been darkened by tragedy and loss. But even as they entertained the idea, they knew that it was a decision that would shape the course of their lives in ways they could scarcely imagine.

With a shared glance, they reached a silent agreement, their hearts entwined in a bond that transcended words. And as they emerged from their private conversation, their smiles held a newfound sense of purpose, a silent promise of the future that lay ahead, a future filled with love, hope, and the endless possibilities of tomorrow.

CHAPTER ELEVEN
SANCTUARY

The morning sun cast a warm glow over the landscape as Erick and his companions emerged from the confines of their sanctuary, the promise of a new day stretching out before them like a blank canvas waiting to be painted. With each step, they carried the weight of their pasts on their shoulders, but also the hope of a brighter future.

As they ventured beyond the safety of their home, the world seemed to come alive around them, vibrant and full of possibility. Birds sang in the treetops, their melodies a joyful refrain that echoed through the forest. The air was crisp and invigorating, carrying with it the scent of pine and earth. Erick breathed deeply, filling his lungs with the sweet fragrance of the wilderness. Beside him, his companions walked in companionable silence, their footsteps echoing in the stillness of the morning. With each passing moment, the tension that had lingered between them began to dissipate, replaced by a sense of unity and purpose. As they ventured further into the wilderness, the landscape unfolded before them in a tapestry of breathtaking beauty. Sunlight filtered through the canopy overhead, dappling the forest floor in a mosaic of light and shadow. The air was alive with the gentle hum of insects and the occasional rustle of leaves, a symphony of nature's song. Erick and his companions walked in reverent silence, their senses alive to the wonders that surrounded them. They marveled at the towering trees that reached towards the sky, their branches swaying gently in the breeze. They paused to admire the delicate beauty of wildflowers that carpeted the forest floor, their vibrant hues a stark contrast against the muted greens and browns of the undergrowth. As they walked, their thoughts turned to the future of their home, to the challenges that lay ahead and the possibilities that awaited them. They spoke of plans for expansion, of building defenses to protect against the dangers that lurked in the shadows. They shared ideas and visions, each one a testament to their unwavering determination to carve out a place of safety and security in a world gone mad.

But amidst the talk of strategy and logistics, there were moments of lightheartedness and laughter, moments of shared joy and camaraderie that served as a reminder of the bond that held them together. They teased and joked, their laughter echoing through the trees like the chiming of bells. As the day wore on, they found themselves drawn deeper into the heart of the forest, their curiosity piqued by the mysteries that lay hidden just beyond their reach. They followed winding paths and babbling brooks, their footsteps guided by a sense of adventure and exploration.

And then, as the sun began its slow descent towards the horizon, they stumbled upon a hidden glade, a secluded oasis nestled amidst the trees. It was a place of rare beauty, untouched by the hand of man, a sanctuary in the heart of the wilderness. With a collective gasp of awe, they entered the glade, their eyes widening in wonder at the sight that greeted them. A crystal-clear stream meandered through the center of the clearing, its waters shimmering in the fading light. Wildflowers bloomed along its banks, their petals kissed by the golden rays of the setting sun.

Without a word, they sank to the ground, their hearts overflowing with gratitude for the simple beauty that surrounded them. They sat in silence, watching as the colors of the sky shifted and changed, painting the world in hues of pink and orange. As the last light of day began to fade, Erick and Alex exchanged a knowing glance, a silent acknowledgment of the dangers lurking in the encroaching darkness. Though they reveled in the serenity of the glade, they remained vigilant, their senses finely attuned to the slightest hint of danger. When they began to walk back towards home the forest seemed to close in around them, shadows lengthening and intertwining like grasping fingers. The air grew thick with tension, a palpable sense of unease settling over the landscape. Suddenly, a low growl pierced the silence, causing Erick's heart to quicken its pace. With a nod from Alex, they both drew their knives, the gleaming blades catching the dim light as they prepared to confront the threat.

"Infected," Alex whispered, his voice barely audible over the rustle of leaves. Erick nodded in agreement, his grip tightening on the handle of his knife as they moved forward, their footsteps muffled by the forest floor. They had faced the infected before, knew their relentless hunger and unpredictable movements all too well. As the first of the infected emerged from the shadows, their eyes glowing with feral hunger, Erick and Alex sprang into action. With a swift and practiced motion, they moved as one, their knives flashing in the darkness as they struck with deadly precision. Each blow landed with a sickening thud to the head, the sound of steel meeting the skull reverberating through the air. The infected lunged and snarled, their movements erratic and unpredictable, but Erick and Alex remained steadfast, their focus unwavering as they danced through the fray. With each fallen adversary, their resolve only strengthened, fueling their determination to protect their home and those they held dear. They fought with a fierce intensity, a silent determination driving them forward even as exhaustion threatened to consume them.

And then, finally, after what felt like an eternity, the last of the infected fell, their bodies crumpling to the forest floor in a grotesque heap. Erick and Alex stood amidst the wreckage, their chests heaving with exertion as they surveyed the aftermath of the battle. In the quiet stillness that followed, they shared a wordless moment of solidarity, their eyes meeting in a silent exchange of understanding. They had faced death head-on and emerged victorious, their bond forged in the crucible of combat stronger than ever before. With a weary sigh, they turned and made their way back to the safety of their sanctuary, their steps heavy with exhaustion but their spirits buoyed by the knowledge that they had prevailed against all odds. And as they disappeared into the darkness of the forest, they knew that no matter what trials may come, they would face them together, a force to be reckoned with in a world gone mad. The fire crackled softly in the hearth, casting flickering shadows across the walls of the dimly lit room. Outside, the night sky stretched out in an expanse of deep indigo, scattered with a myriad of stars that twinkled like distant diamonds. The hour was late, long past midnight, yet the members of the group remained gathered together, their voices a low murmur as they spoke in hushed tones. They sat huddled around the table, their faces illuminated by the warm glow of candlelight, their expressions drawn with weariness but also with a sense of camaraderie that bound them together. Erick stirred on the couch, his eyes fluttering open as he roused from a fitful nap. He blinked groggily, his mind still foggy from sleep as he took in the scene before him. His companions spoke in quiet tones, their voices a soothing backdrop to the stillness of the night. With a yawn, Erick pushed himself upright, his muscles protesting the sudden movement after hours of restless slumber. He ran a hand through his tousled hair, his gaze drifting over to where his mother sat, her eyes tired but filled with a quiet strength that never wavered.

As he joined the group at the table, the conversation ebbed and flowed around him, a comforting presence in the otherwise silent night. But even as they spoke, Erick couldn't shake the feeling of unease that gnawed at his gut. Erick's heart pounded in his chest as the memories of that fateful night flooded back, the events playing out before his eyes like a vivid nightmare. He could still hear the screams echoing through the darkness, could still feel the weight of his father's revolver in his hands as he stumbled upon the scene.

With a heavy heart, Erick turned to Alex, his voice barely a whisper. "It was my father... He killed the boy." Alex's eyes widened in shock, his grip tightening on his deck of playing cards as he processed Erick's words. "Are you sure?" he asked, his voice tinged with disbelief. Erick nodded solemnly, his gaze fixed on the ground as he struggled to contain the flood of emotions threatening to overwhelm him."I saw it with my own eyes," he replied, his voice trembling with emotion. "He was trying to protect us, but... he lost control." The weight of the revelation hung heavy in the air, casting a shadow over their already heavy hearts. For a long moment, they sat in silence, grappling with the magnitude of what Erick had revealed.

As the night wore on, laughter and conversation filled the room, a welcome reprieve from the weight of the world outside. Erick and his companions gathered around the table, the flickering candlelight casting a warm glow over their faces as they settled in for a long game of poker. The cards shuffled and dealt, the clinking of chips and the occasional burst of laughter punctuating the air as they played. They traded jokes and stories, their voices rising and falling in a symphony of camaraderie. Erick's mother smiled fondly as she watched her son and his companions, her heart swelling with pride at the bond they shared. Despite the hardships they had faced, they remained resilient, finding joy and solace in each other's company. As the game stretched on into the night, the hour grew late, and one by one, the players began to retire to their beds. Erick stifled a yawn as he bid his companions goodnight, exhaustion tugging at his eyelids as he made his way to his room.

Meanwhile, Alex and Vanessa lingered behind, their fingers intertwined as they shared a knowing glance. With a silent nod, they rose from the table, their steps light as they ascended the stairs to their room. Once inside, they closed the door behind them, the quiet of the night enveloping them like a comforting blanket. With a tender smile, Alex pulled Vanessa into his arms, their bodies pressed close as they shared a moment of quiet intimacy. In the soft glow of candlelight, they whispered words of love and devotion, their hearts beating in sync as they reveled in the closeness they shared. And as they surrendered to the warmth of each other's embrace, they knew that their love would carry them through whatever trials may come, lighting the way to a future filled with hope and possibility. The night hung heavy with silence as Vanessa stirred in her room, her movements careful and deliberate as she slipped out of bed.

The soft glow of moonlight filtered through the curtains, casting long shadows across the floor as she tiptoed towards the bathroom to go pee, careful not to disturb the others who slept soundly in the adjoining rooms.

As she reached the bathroom door, a glint of light caught her eye, drawing her attention to the open medicine cabinet. With a furrowed brow, she peered inside, her heart skipping a beat as she caught sight of a small box tucked away at the back. Curiosity piqued, Vanessa reached for the box, her fingers trembling slightly as she pulled it out from its hiding place. Her breath caught in her throat as she read the label, her mind racing with a thousand thoughts and emotions. With a shaky exhale, she tore open the box and retrieved the pregnancy test nestled inside. Her hands shook as she followed the instructions, her heart pounding in her chest as she waited for the results to appear.

Seconds stretched into eternity as Vanessa stared at the test, her breath coming in shallow gasps as she watched the faint pink lines begin to materialize. And then, in a rush of overwhelming emotion, she collapsed to the floor, tears streaming down her cheeks as she processed the life-altering news. With trembling hands, Vanessa rose to her feet, her mind a whirlwind of disbelief and joy. She took a moment to compose herself before quietly slipping out of the bathroom, her heart racing with anticipation as she made her way back to the room where Alex slept.

As she entered the room, she found Alex stirring awake, his eyes heavy with sleep as he watched her approach.

Without a word, she climbed back into bed beside him, her heart pounding in her chest as she took his hand in hers.

"Alex," she whispered, her voice barely more than a breath as she met his gaze. "I... I'm pregnant." She stuttered a little trying to get that one out. Alex's eyes widened in shock, his hand flying to his mouth to stifle a gasp of disbelief. But then, as the reality of the moment sank in, a smile spread across his face, his eyes shining with unshed tears.

"Oh, Vanessa," he murmured, his voice choked with emotion as he pulled her close.

"This is... this is incredible." With tears of joy streaming down their faces, they held each other tight, their hearts overflowing with love and gratitude for the miracle that awaited them. And as they drifted off to sleep, their hands intertwined and their hearts entwined, they knew that their lives would never be the same again, filled with the boundless promise of a future filled with love, laughter, and the pitter-patter of tiny feet.

CHAPTER TWELVE
BOUND BY LOVE

The morning sun painted the sky in hues of rose and gold as a sense of anticipation hung heavy in the air. In the sanctuary that had become their home, Erick and his companions awoke to a new day, each heart brimming with the promise of what lay ahead.

As the first light filtered through the windows, casting soft shadows across the room, Vanessa stirred in bed, her hand instinctively reaching for the swell of her belly. Beside her, Alex slept soundly, his arm draped protectively over her as if to shield her from the world. With a smile, Vanessa traced a gentle finger along the curve of her stomach, feeling the flutter of life within. She marveled at the miracle growing inside her, a testament to the love she shared with Alex and the hope they held for the future.

As she lay there, lost in thoughts of the life growing within her, the room began to stir with activity. Erick's mother bustled about, preparing breakfast with a sense of purpose that spoke volumes of her determination to care for her new family. Erick emerged from his room, rubbing sleep from his eyes as he greeted the morning with a yawn. His gaze lingered on Vanessa and Alex, a smile tugging at the corners of his lips as he took in the sight of the happy couple.

"Morning," he yawned, rubbing his eyes, his voice warm with affection as he joined them at the table. "How are you feeling, Vanessa?" Vanessa's smile widened at the concern in Erick's voice, a swell of gratitude washing over her. "I'm feeling... amazing," she replied, her hand drifting once more to her belly. "Thank you."

As they sat down to breakfast, the air was alive with the hum of conversation, the room filled with laughter and camaraderie. They spoke of plans for the day ahead, of chores to be done and supplies to be gathered, but beneath it all, there lingered a sense of excitement for the future. Vanessa and Alex stood side by side, their hands intertwined as they exchanged nervous glances. This moment had been weighing heavily on their minds, the weight of the news they carried threatening to overwhelm them. With a deep breath, Vanessa stepped forward, her heart pounding in her chest as she addressed the group. "Everyone," she began, her voice trembling slightly with emotion. "There's something we need to tell you." The room fell silent as all eyes turned to Vanessa and Alex, their expressions a mixture of curiosity and concern. Erick's mother reached out, her hand resting gently on Vanessa's arm in a silent gesture of support. Taking strength from the reassuring touch, Vanessa continued, her words tumbling out in a rush as she struggled to find the right ones to convey the magnitude of what she was about to reveal.

"Alex and I" She paused for a second or two, before continuing, "we're going to have a baby."

A gasp rippled through the room as the news sank in, the air electric with a mixture of shock and joy. Erick's eyes widened in disbelief, his mouth forming a silent 'wow' as he took in the enormity of the revelation. Erick's mother let out a soft cry of happiness, tears glistening in her eyes as she pulled Vanessa into a tight embrace. "Oh, my dear," she whispered, her voice thick with emotion. "This is wonderful news."

The rest of the group erupted into cheers and applause, their voices blending together in a chorus of celebration. They surrounded Vanessa and Alex, enveloping them in a sea of love and support as they offered their congratulations.

Amidst the jubilation, Vanessa felt a surge of overwhelming emotion wash over her. Tears pricked at her eyes as she looked around at the faces of her friends and family, their smiles reflecting the joy that filled her heart.

The fire crackled softly in the hearth, casting dancing shadows across the room as Alex and Vanessa sat together on the worn couch, their faces illuminated by the warm glow of candlelight. Outside, the night pressed in around them, the darkness a stark reminder of the dangers that lurked beyond the safety of their sanctuary. Silent for a moment, they sat lost in thought, the weight of their impending parenthood heavy on their minds. Vanessa chewed nervously on her lower lip, her eyes fixed on the flickering flames as she struggled to find the right words.

Finally, breaking the silence, Alex spoke, his voice low and hesitant. "Vanessa, I... I know this is a lot to take in. The world out there is... it's dangerous, especially for a newborn." Vanessa nodded, her heart heavy with worry as she considered the risks they would face. "I know," she replied, her voice barely more than a whisper. "But... but I can't help but feel hopeful, too. Maybe bringing a child into this world is exactly what we need to find hope again." Alex reached out, his hand finding hers in the dim light of the room. "I understand, Vanessa. I do. But I can't shake this feeling of... of fear. What if we can't protect them? What if something happens?" Vanessa squeezed his hand reassuringly, her eyes meeting his in a silent exchange of understanding. "We'll do whatever it takes to keep our child safe, Alex. Together, we're stronger than anything this world can throw at us." They sat in quiet contemplation, the weight of their conversation hanging heavy in the air. Outside, the wind whispered through the trees, a haunting reminder of the world beyond their walls.

And yet, despite the uncertainty that lay ahead, Vanessa felt a sense of peace settle over her. In that moment, surrounded by the warmth of Alex's love, she knew that no matter what challenges they may face, they would face them together, bound by the unbreakable bond of family and the infinite power of love.

CHAPTER THIRTEEN
PREPARING FOR WINTER

The first light of dawn filtered through the windows of the sanctuary, casting a light glow over the room where Erick and his companions slept. As the group stirred awake, a sense of purpose hung heavy in the air, mingling with the anticipation of what lay ahead. Vanessa and Alex were the first to rise, their minds already abuzz with plans and preparations for the arrival of their baby. They moved about the room with a sense of determination, their steps purposeful as they gathered their belongings and prepared to face the day. Erick watched them from across the room, a small smile playing at the corners of his lips as he observed the quiet intensity with which they worked. He knew that the road ahead would be difficult, filled with challenges and uncertainties, but he also knew that Vanessa and Alex were more than up to the task. As the rest of the group began to rouse from their slumber, the room quickly filled with activity. Erick's mother bustled about, preparing breakfast with a sense of urgency that spoke volumes of her determination to ensure that her family was well-fed and cared for.

Outside, the sounds of the morning echoed through the air, the chirping of birds and the rustle of leaves a soothing backdrop to the hustle and bustle within the sanctuary.

As autumn faded into winter, the group found themselves faced with the daunting task of preparing for the harsh months ahead. With the biting cold already creeping in, they knew that they would need to take every precaution to ensure their survival in the unforgiving landscape outside. Erick and Alex took charge of fortifying the sanctuary, reinforcing the walls and windows to keep out the cold and any unwanted visitors. They worked tirelessly, their muscles aching with exertion as they labored late into the night, driven by a fierce determination to protect their makeshift home and the ones they loved.

Meanwhile, Vanessa and Erick's mother busied themselves with gathering supplies, stockpiling food, water, and firewood to see them through the long winter months. They scoured the surrounding area for any resources they could find, their efforts fueled by a sense of urgency and the knowledge that their survival depended on it.

As the days grew shorter and the nights grew colder, the group came together to share warmth and companionship in the face of adversity. They gathered around the fire, their laughter and chatter echoing through the room as they exchanged stories and shared memories of days gone by. But beneath the surface, there was an undercurrent of unease, a sense of foreboding that lingered in the air like a dark shadow. The world outside was a dangerous place, filled with unknown dangers and unseen threats, and they knew that they would need to remain vigilant if they were to survive.

As they prepared for the challenges that lay ahead, the group found solace in each other's company, drawing strength from their shared bond and the knowledge that together, they could overcome whatever obstacles came their way.

CHAPTER FOURTEEN
COLD

Three and a half months later in the depths of winter, a bitter cold gripped the sanctuary, its icy fingers seeping through the cracks in the walls and chilling the bones of its inhabitants. Despite their best efforts to stay warm and healthy, illness lingered like a shadow, waiting to strike when least expected.

One day, Erick noticed a change in his mother's demeanor. She seemed more tired than usual, her usually vibrant energy subdued by a persistent cough and a hint of fatigue in her eyes. At first, they brushed it off as nothing more than a passing cold, a minor inconvenience in the grand scheme of their survival. But as the days passed, Christa's condition worsened. The cough grew more persistent, rattling her chest with each breath, and her once boundless energy waned, leaving her weak and listless. Despite her efforts to hide it, Erick could see the strain etched into her features, the worry that creased her brow whenever she thought no one was looking. Concerned for his mother's well-being, Erick urged her to rest and take care of herself. But Christa, ever the pillar of strength, brushed off his concerns with a reassuring smile, insisting that she was fine and that there were more pressing matters to attend to.

As the days turned into weeks, however, it became increasingly clear that something was seriously wrong. Christa's cough grew more severe, her breathing labored as she struggled to draw in each breath. Fever raged through her body, leaving her weak and delirious as she drifted in and out of consciousness. Despite their best efforts, there was little they could do to halt the progression of the illness. Erick watched helplessly as his mother's condition worsened, his heart heavy with worry and fear for her well-being.

In her final moments, surrounded by her son and their makeshift family, Christa slipped peacefully into eternal slumber, her battle with illness finally at an end. Her passing left a void in Erick's heart, a gaping wound that would never fully heal. But amidst the pain and sorrow, there was also a sense of gratitude for the time they had shared, and a determination to honor her memory by carrying on her legacy of strength, resilience, and unwavering love. But Erick had to finish it, before she turned. Everybody left the room and gave them space. As the flickering flames of the hearth cast shadows over the room, the group gathered around Christa's resting place, their hearts heavy with grief. Erick's mother, the matriarch of their makeshift family, had been a beacon of strength and resilience, guiding them through the darkest of times with her unwavering love and resolve. Tears streamed down Vanessa's cheeks as she clutched Alex's hand tightly, her heart aching with sorrow for the loss of their dear friend and mentor. Alex held her close, offering what little comfort he could as they mourned the passing of a woman who had become a mother to both of them. Erick stood beside them, his gaze fixed on his mother's still form, a lump forming in his throat as he struggled to find the words to express the depth of his grief. Memories of happier times flooded his mind, of moments shared and lessons learned, each one a testament to the profound impact his mother had had on his life.

As the hours stretched on into the night, the group remained huddled together, drawing strength from each other as they navigated the turbulent waters of grief. They shared stories and memories of Christa, each one a bittersweet reminder of the love and warmth she had brought into their lives. And as they lay down to rest that night, their hearts heavy with sorrow yet filled with a quiet resolve, they knew that Christa's legacy would live on in the bonds of friendship and love that bound them together. Though she was gone, her spirit would remain with them always, a guiding light in the darkness, leading them forward on their journey of survival and hope.

CHAPTER FIFTEEN
I THINK IT'S TIME

The sanctuary basked in the soft hues of a spring morning, with the gentle warmth of April sunlight filtering through the windows, casting a golden glow over the room. But amidst the tranquility of the season's awakening, a palpable sense of anticipation lingered, blending seamlessly with the soft chirping of birds outside. Inside, Vanessa awoke with a start, a sudden discomfort seizing her body. She shifted restlessly in bed, one hand instinctively cradling her burgeoning belly as she attempted to decipher the sensation coursing through her. Beside her, Alex stirred from his slumber, his brow furrowing in concern as he registered her distress. "Vanessa, what's wrong?" he inquired, his voice tinged with worry.

Vanessa nodded, her breath catching as another wave of discomfort washed over her. "I... I think it's time," she managed to utter, her voice strained with effort. With a sense of urgency, Alex sprang into action, his movements swift and purposeful as he assisted Vanessa in rising from bed. Together, they made their way to the common area, where Erick had already gathered, drawn by the commotion.

As Vanessa settled into a small makeshift bed, the two guys converged around her, offering words of encouragement and support as they readied themselves for what lay ahead. Erick's presence was a source of strength and comfort, his unwavering support a reassuring presence in this moment of need.

Outside, the world seemed to hold its breath, as if in anticipation of the new life about to emerge. Inside the sanctuary, time appeared to stand still as Vanessa labored, her strength and resolve a testament to the profound love she held for her unborn child.

Hours passed, each one marked by the rhythmic ebb and flow of Vanessa's contractions. The group remained steadfast at her side, offering comfort and reassurance as she navigated the intensity of childbirth with grace and fortitude.

And then, finally, as the sun dipped below the horizon, a cry broke through the stillness of the room, heralding the arrival of new life. Tears of joy welled in As Vanessa cradled her newborn child in her arms, tears of joy streaming down her cheeks, she couldn't help but marvel at the tiny bundle of life nestled against her chest. With a soft coo, the baby stirred, their eyes fluttering open to reveal a pair of bright, curious eyes.

"It's a girl," Alex whispered, his voice filled with awe and wonder as he gazed down at his daughter, his heart overflowing with love for the precious new addition to their family. Vanessa smiled through her tears, her heart swelling with pride as she looked down at her daughter. "Welcome to the world, little one," she murmured, pressing a gentle kiss to the baby's forehead.

As the night descended upon the sanctuary, the group gathered around Vanessa and baby Emily, their hearts full of joy and gratitude for the precious gift of new life. They shared stories and laughter, their spirits buoyed by the promise of the future and the strength of their bonds.

Outside, the world continued to spin on, oblivious to the tiny miracle that had taken place within the sanctuary's walls. But inside, amidst the flickering glow of candlelight and the soft lullaby of a newborn's coos, time seemed to stand still, as if to savor the beauty of this fleeting moment of peace and happiness. Together, they named her Emily, a name that held significance and meaning for both of them, a symbol of hope and new beginnings in a world filled with uncertainty.

CHAPTER SIXTEEN
ADIEU

Eight years had slipped by like grains of sand through an hourglass, each moment filled with the joys and challenges of life in the post-apocalyptic world. In that time, Vanessa, Alex, and Erick had nurtured and watched over Emily as she blossomed from a newborn into a spirited young girl. Together, they had formed an unbreakable bond, forged in the crucible of their shared experiences and the love that bound them together. The sanctuary had grown in size and strength over the years, expanding to accommodate the growing number of survivors who sought refuge within its walls. What had once been a humble shelter now stood as a beacon of hope in the desolate landscape, offering safety and sanctuary to those in need.

Under Erick's leadership, the group had worked tirelessly to fortify their home, building additional walls and defenses to protect against the ever-present threat of the infected and other dangers that lurked beyond their borders. They had also expanded their resources, cultivating crops and raising livestock to sustain themselves in the harsh new world they inhabited.

But amidst the challenges of survival, there had also been moments of joy and camaraderie. The group had welcomed new members into their fold, forming bonds of friendship and kinship that transcended the boundaries of blood. Together, they had shared laughter and tears, victories and defeats, finding strength and solace in each other's company.

As Emily raced through the corridors of the sanctuary, her laughter echoing through the air, Vanessa, Erick, and Alex watched with pride and wonder, marveling at the resilient spirit of the young girl who had brought so much light into their lives. And as they looked to the future, they knew that no matter what may come, they would face it together, united by their unwavering love for each other and the hope that burned bright within their hearts.

As the sun dipped below the horizon, casting long shadows across the sanctuary, Vanessa, Erick, Alex, and Emily gathered around the communal fire pit, their faces illuminated by the flickering flames. Joining them were several other members of their group, each with their own story to tell. One of the newcomers was Marcus, a grizzled veteran of the old world who had found his way to the sanctuary in search of refuge. He sat beside Erick, his weathered features softened by the warmth of the fire as he spoke.

Marcus: "Back in the day, I used to be a mechanic. Never thought I'd be fixing up old cars just to keep 'em running in this world." Erick nodded in understanding, a sense of camaraderie forming between them as they shared stories of their past lives and the struggles they faced in the present. Nearby, a young woman named Lily tended to the fire, her gentle demeanor belying the inner strength that had carried her through the darkest of times.

Lily: "I used to be a teacher before all of this. Never imagined I'd be learning how to grow vegetables and fend off the infected just to survive." Vanessa smiled warmly at her, grateful for her presence and the sense of normalcy she brought to their makeshift family.

Meanwhile, a group of children played nearby, their laughter mingling with the crackling of the fire as they chased each other around in a game of tag.

Emily: "Come on, let's play!" The children's infectious energy brought a smile to everyone's faces, a reminder of the resilience of youth and the hope that burned bright within their hearts.

As the night settled around the sanctuary, casting long shadows over the gathered group, Erick's gaze lingered on a figure sitting on the outskirts of the firelight. He rose from his seat and made his way over to her, a sense of unease gnawing at his gut. Sitting beside the woman, whose name was Sofia, Erick felt a wave of guilt wash over him. Sofia was a recent addition to their group, having arrived at the sanctuary seeking refuge from the dangers of the outside world. In her eyes, he saw a reflection of his own pain and longing for connection.

Erick: "Sofia, we need to talk." Sofia turned to him, her expression a mixture of curiosity and apprehension. "What is it, Erick?" Taking a deep breath, Erick struggled to find the right words to convey the turmoil raging within him. "I... I think it's time we talked about ourselves. About what this... what we have." Sofia's eyes widened in surprise, a flicker of hope dancing in their depths. "You mean..." Erick nodded, his heart heavy with the weight of his confession. "I care about you, Sofia. More than I ever thought possible after... after everything." Sofia reached out and took his hand in hers, her touch sending a shiver down Erick's spine. "I care about you too, Erick. More than you know."

Their conversation was interrupted by a soft voice calling out from the darkness. "Daddy, can I sit with you?" Turning, Erick saw his son, a boy of four years old named Lucas, standing shyly behind them, his eyes wide with curiosity. Erick's heart swelled with love for the young boy, his presence a reminder of the preciousness of life in a world filled with darkness and uncertainty. Erick: "Of course, Lucas. Come sit with us."

As the night continued, Erick, Sofia, and Lucas sat together by the fire, their hearts intertwined in a bond of love and hope for the future. Then, with a solemn tone, Erick stood up, drawing the attention of the group once more.

"Erick, what's going on?" Vanessa asked, concern etched on her face." Taking a moment to collect his thoughts, Erick spoke with conviction, his voice carrying through the stillness of the night.

"I have something important to share with all of you," he began. "Sofia and I have made contact with a community called Haven's Reach."

"Haven's Reach?" Alex echoed, his brow furrowed in confusion. "Where is that?"

"It's several days' journey from here," Erick explained, his gaze sweeping over the faces of his companions. "But it's a place of safety, with leaders and an army that will protect us." A murmur of disbelief rippled through the group, mingling with the crackling of the fire. Vanessa's eyes widened with hope, while Emily clung tightly to her father's hand, sensing the weight of his words. "We are leaving in the morning," Erick continued, his voice steady but tinged with emotion. "To seek refuge with Haven's Reach, for the sake of our family." Tears welled up in Vanessa's eyes as she stepped forward, enveloping Erick and Sofia in a tight embrace. "We'll miss you," she whispered, her voice choked with emotion. "But we understand." Alex nodded solemnly, his expression mirroring Vanessa's sentiments. "You have to do what's best for your family," he said, his voice thick with emotion.

Emily stood beside them, her eyes brimming with tears as she struggled to find the words to express her feelings. "I'll miss you both," she said softly, her voice trembling with emotion. "But I know you'll be safe." As the reality of their impending departure sank in, the group gathered around Erick

As the sun rose higher in the sky, casting long shadows across the sanctuary, Erick, Sofia, and Lucas emerged from the shelter, their chosen vehicle awaiting them—a sturdy truck that the group had prepared for their journey to Haven's Reach. The engine roared to life, echoing through the silent morning as they loaded their belongings into the back. The group gathered around the vehicle, their faces solemn as they exchanged final words of farewell. Tears glistened in Vanessa's eyes as she hugged Erick and Sofia tightly, her voice choked with emotion. "Take care of each other," she whispered, her words a heartfelt plea.

Erick nodded, his own eyes shimmering with unshed tears. "We will," he promised, his voice filled with determination. Alex clasped Erick's shoulder in a silent gesture of support, his expression grave. "Stay safe out there," he said, his voice gruff with emotion. "And know that you're always welcome back here."

Emily stood beside them, her small hand clutching Sofia's tightly. "I don't want you to go," she admitted, her voice trembling with emotion. Sofia knelt down beside her, wrapping her arms around the young girl in a comforting embrace. "I know, sweetie," she murmured, her own eyes brimming with tears. "But we'll always be with you, no matter where we are. With one last round of hugs and tearful goodbyes, Erick, Sofia, and Lucas climbed into the truck, their hearts heavy with the weight of their parting. The engine roared to life once more, drowning out the sound of their friends' farewells as they drove off into the horizon, leaving behind only memories and the promise of a brighter tomorrow.

CHAPTER SEVENTEEN
REMEMBERANCE

Fifteen years had passed since the untimely deaths of Vanessa and Alex, the heart and soul of the sanctuary. Their absence lingered like a shadow over the once vibrant community, casting a pall of sorrow that refused to dissipate with the passing of time. Emily, now twenty-nine years old and weathered by the harsh realities of the post-apocalyptic world, stood amidst the bustling activity of the abandoned sanctuary, her heart heavy with both grief and determination.

The memory of their deaths haunted her still, a painful reminder of the fragility of life in a world fraught with danger and uncertainty. It had happened suddenly, without warning, on a routine expedition beyond the sanctuary walls. Vanessa and Alex had been leading a small group in search of much-needed supplies when tragedy struck. A horde of infected had descended upon them with terrifying speed, overwhelming their defenses in a matter of moments. In the chaos that ensued, Vanessa and Alex had fought bravely to protect their companions, but in the end, they had been outnumbered and outmatched. The sanctuary had received word of their deaths only hours later, a devastating blow that had left the entire community reeling in shock and disbelief. But amidst the despair, a glimmer of hope emerged from an unexpected source. The Haven's Reach militia, a formidable force known for their expertise in combating the infected, had arrived on the scene just in time to stem the tide of the horde. With their advanced weaponry and strategic prowess, they had managed to push back the infected and secure the area, but it was too late for Vanessa and Alex. In the aftermath of the battle, the survivors of the sanctuary were welcomed into the safety of Haven's Reach, their wounded hearts finding solace in the warmth and security of their new home. And amidst the chaos of their arrival, Emily found her place among the ranks of the Haven's Reach militia, her strength and determination earning her a reputation as one of their most formidable soldiers.

But what shocked Emily and the others even more was the revelation that Erick, now fifty-nine years old, had risen to the esteemed position of commander within the Haven's Reach militia. The quiet and unassuming man they had known from years past had transformed into a formidable leader, his wisdom and tactical brilliance guiding the mili- tia to countless victories against the infected and other threats. As she stood now, clad in armor and armed to the teeth, Emily couldn't help but marvel at the journey that had brought them all here. Gone were the days of innocence and naivety, replaced by the cold, hard realities of life in a world torn apart by chaos and despair. But with each passing day, they grew stronger and more resilient, their resolve unwavering in the face of adversity.

As the sun dipped below the horizon, casting long shadows over the sanctuary-turned-refugee camp, Emily stood tall amidst her comrades-in-arms, a sense of peace settling over her weary heart. In the face of loss and hardship, they had forged a new beginning, their spirits undaunted by the trials that lay ahead. And as they looked to the future, united in their resolve and bound by the ties of kinship, they knew that they would face whatever challenges came their way with courage and determination. For in the end, it was not just survival that mattered, but the strength of the human spirit to endure, to rebuild, and to thrive once more in a world forever changed by *The Reckoning.*

Turn the page for an *exclusive* sneak peek of

THE RECKONING
EMILY'S JOURNEY

Book two in Jayden Carlisle's *The Reckoning* series!

Chapter 1

The crunch of gravel underfoot echoed through the abandoned streets as I moved stealthily, my senses alert to the slightest sign of danger. Ahead, the crumbling facades of once-grand buildings loomed like silent sentinels, their hollow windows staring back at me with vacant eyes. Beside me, the soft murmur of my comrades' voices provided a reassuring anchor in the eerie silence of the city. We moved as one, a well-oiled machine honed by years of survival in a world overrun by the infected. My grip tightened on the handle of my rifle as we approached a particularly desolate intersection, our eyes scanning the shadows for any sign of movement. The air hung heavy with anticipation, each breath a whispered prayer for safety in a world where danger lurked around every corner. Suddenly, a faint rustling sound broke the silence, sending a jolt of adrenaline coursing through my veins. Instinct took over as I signaled for my team to halt, my senses on high alert as I scanned the surrounding buildings for any sign of threat. A flicker of movement caught my eye, and I tensed, ready to spring into action at a moment's notice. But as the figure emerged from the shadows, relief washed over me like a wave crashing against the shore.

"It's just a stray dog," I muttered under my breath, my heart still racing from the adrenaline rush of the moment. Beside me, my companions let out a collective sigh of relief, their tense expressions softening as the tension slowly ebbed away. With a silent nod, we resumed our journey through the deserted streets, our mission clear in our minds. We were scouts, tasked with venturing beyond the safety of Haven's Reach to gather supplies and gather intelligence on the migrations of the infected. As we pressed on, I couldn't help but marvel at the resilience of the human spirit, even in the face of such overwhelming adversity. Despite the dangers that lurked around every corner, we refused to be cowed into submission, determined to carve out a new existence in a world forever changed by *the reckoning*.

As the sun dipped below the horizon, casting long shadows over the desolate landscape, I knew that our fight with the infected was far from over. The desolate streets stretched on, seemingly endless in their decay. We moved with purpose, our footsteps echoing off the broken pavement, a stark reminder of the emptiness that surrounded us. But despite the bleakness of our surroundings, a sense of determination burned bright within me, driving me forward with unwavering resolve. Whilst we navigated through the labyrinthine streets, our senses remained on high alert, every shadow and every sound scrutinized for signs of danger. The scent of decay hung heavy in the air, mingling with the faint hint of smoke that lingered from distant fires.

Suddenly, a faint shuffling sound echoed from an adjacent alleyway, causing me to freeze in my tracks. I raised a hand, signaling for my companions to halt as I strained to identify the source of the noise. My heart pounded in my chest as I gripped my rifle tighter, my muscles tensed and ready for anything. With cautious steps, I edged closer to the alley, my senses on high alert for any sign of movement. As I rounded the corner, my breath caught in my throat as I came face to face with a small group of infected. Their sunken eyes glinted with hunger as they lurched towards me, their decaying bodies moving with an unnatural gait. Without hesitation, I raised my rifle and took aim, my finger tightened on the trigger as I prepared to defend myself. The crack of gunfire shattered the silence, echoing through the empty streets as I opened fire on the approaching horde. Bullets tore through the air, finding their mark with deadly accuracy as the infected fell one by one, their lifeless bodies crumpling to the ground in a heap. But even as I fought back the tide of undead, I knew that this struggle was far from over. More infected poured into the alleyway, drawn by the sound of gunfire like moths to a porch light. We were outnumbered and outmatched, our only hope of survival resting on our ability to hold them off long enough to make our escape. Gritting my teeth, I fought with a ferocity born of desperation, every movement fueled by the need to protect my comrades and ensure our survival. But as the horde closed in around us, I knew that our fate hung in the balance, teetering on the knife's edge between life and death. With a final burst of adrenaline, we fought our way free from the grasp of the infected, racing through the streets with the sound of their anguished cries echoing in our ears. And as we emerged into the safety of the open road, I couldn't help but marvel at the fragility of life in a world torn apart by chaos and despair. But amidst the chaos, a glimmer of hope emerged, a determination to persevere against all odds.

We fled from the rest of the horde, our hearts pounding with the intensity of our escape, a deafening roar shattered the air, shaking the ground beneath our feet. I stumbled, nearly losing my balance as the shockwave rippled through the streets, sending debris flying in all directions. With a sinking feeling in the pit of my stomach, I turned to see a plume of smoke rising in the distance, billowing into the sky like a dark omen of destruction. Dread washed over me like a tidal wave as the realization sank in:

our home was under attack. Without hesitation, I urged my companions to follow as we raced back towards the heart of the city, our minds racing with fear and uncertainty. Every step felt like a mile as we pushed through the throngs of panicked survivors, their anguished cries echoing in our ears.

As we reached the outskirts of Haven's Reach, the full extent of the devastation came into view. Buildings lay in ruins, their charred remains smoldering in the aftermath of the attack. The air was thick with the acrid scent of smoke and ash, choking off our breath as we surveyed the destruction wrought upon our once-vibrant community. My heart constricted with grief as I searched desperately for any sign of life amidst the rubble, praying for some semblance of hope in the face of such overwhelming despair. But all around me, there was only death and destruction, a grim testament to the fragility of life in a world torn apart by death. Tears stung my eyes as I stumbled through the wreckage, my hands trembling with a mixture of rage and sorrow. How could this have happened? Who could have orchestrated such a heinous act of violence against innocent survivors?

But amidst the devastation, a flicker of movement caught my eye, drawing my gaze towards a figure huddled amidst the ruins. With a surge of hope, I rushed forward, my heart pounding in my chest as I reached out to offer what little comfort I could. As I knelt beside the survivor, I recoiled in horror at the sight before me. Their body was twisted and broken, their face contorted in agony as they gasped for breath amidst the rubble. Blood seeped from countless wounds, staining the ground beneath them with a grim reminder of the brutality of the attack. In that moment, the full weight of our reality came crashing down upon me like a ton of bricks. We were not safe. We were not untouchable. Even the strongest among us could fall victim to the horrors that lurked in the shadows.

But amidst the pain and the sorrow, a fire ignited within me, burning with a fierce determination to seek justice for those we had lost. For in the face of such unspeakable tragedy, there could be no room for despair. Only action. Only vengeance. And as I stood amidst the ruins of our home, I knew that our fight was far from over. For in the face of death and destruction, we would rise from the ashes, stronger and more resilient than ever before. And together, we will take back what we had lost, we will get revenge. And this is *just* the beginning.